The subject matt
vocabulary have
with expert assist
brief and simple text is printed
in large, clear type.

Children's questions are
anticipated and facts presented
in a logical sequence. Where
possible, the books show
what happened in the past
and what is relevant today.

Special artwork has been
commissioned to set a standard
rarely seen in books for this
reading age and at this price.

Full-colour illustrations are on
all 48 pages to give maximum
impact and provide the
extra enrichment that is the
aim of all Ladybird Leaders.

List of contents

A Ladybird Leader

trains

written by David Carey

illustrated by Martin Aitchison, Gerald Witcomb,
Robert Ayton and John Berry

A train pulled by a horse

This was the first public railway
in the world.

A horse could pull more wagons
on rails than it could on a road.

*The Surrey Iron Railway
opened in 1803.*

4

A famous early steam locomotive

The first steam locomotive
was built in 1804.
In 1829 Stephenson built 'The Rocket'.
It could pull a full load
at 24 miles an hour.
The 'Age of Steam' on the railways
had begun.

The Liverpool and Manchester Railway

First class carriages

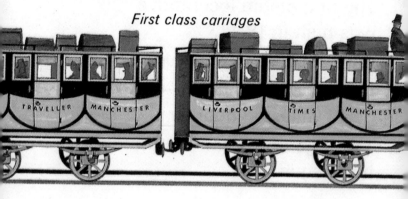

This was the first public railway
using only steam locomotives
and no horses.

At its opening in 1830,
a Member of Parliament was
run down and killed by a locomotive.

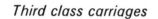

Third class carriages

7

Bigger locomotives — heavier loads

About fifty years later, locomotives
and wagons looked like this.

The engines were more powerful
and could pull much greater loads.

Greater comfort — longer journeys

Large main line stations were built.

The carriages were more comfortable.

Because carriages were comfortable, people made long journeys more often.

Comfort for a Queen

Here is a very comfortable coach.
It was the one Queen Victoria rode in.
Inside, it was furnished like a room
in a house.

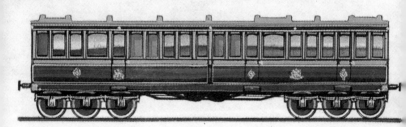

Early American locomotives

This engine did not burn coal.
It burned wood.
It had a 'cow-catcher' at the front
to push away animals.

This was another
early American locomotive.
It burned coal.

The joining of the Union Pacific and Central Pacific railways

After these railways met in 1869,
people could travel by rail
right across America.

The first big railway accident

In 1879 the Tay bridge, in Scotland,
collapsed in a gale.

A mail train and 80 people
fell into the water.

A giant steam locomotive

The 'Big Boy' Union Pacific engines were some of the biggest ever built.

They were a hundred times heavier than 'The Rocket'.

'The Mallard' was the fastest
steam locomotive in the world.
In 1938 it reached 126 miles an hour.

Railways that climb steep hills

On this steep railway,
cables connect two 'cars'.
The 'car' going down
      helps to pull the other one up.

This railway has a toothed rack between the rails.

Under the engine, a toothed wheel turns in the rack.

This pulls the train up steep slopes where the other wheels would slip.

Small trains

This train is pulled by a model
of a famous American locomotive.
Children have fun riding on it.
It is called
The Hoot, Toot and Whistle Railway.

This small train
travels in a tunnel under London.
It carries mail for the Post Office.
The train runs without a driver.

Trains that carry cars

Special trains take new cars
from the car factories.
One train can carry as many cars
as twenty car transporters on the road.

Trains that go by sea

Some ships are built
to carry whole trains across the sea.
The train is driven on to the ship.
These ships are called train ferries.

Special freight trains

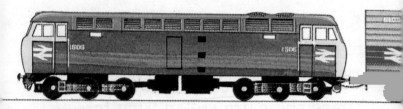

Some goods are put in big boxes.
These boxes are called containers.
Trains take them to the docks.
Cranes lift them on to special ships.

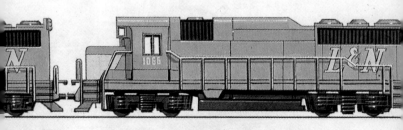

A container train.

In Australia, sheep are carried
in special trucks 85 feet (25.9 m) long.
Five locomotives are linked
to pull some American coal trains.
Each truck (hopper) holds 100 tons.

An American coal train.

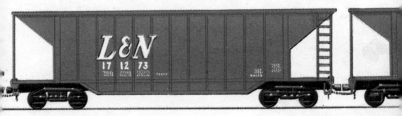

A railway across Australia

The Indian-Pacific Railway crosses
Australia from the Indian Ocean
to the Pacific Ocean.
It runs from Perth to Sydney
and is more than 2,000 miles long.

A railway across Canada

Every day, 'The Canadian' train
runs right across Canada, from
Montreal and Toronto to Vancouver.
The train has two cars with domes.
These give the best possible views.

A railway under the ground

Some cities have underground trains.
Without them, there would be
much more traffic on the city roads.

London has 252 miles
of underground railway.

Another sort of underground railway

This is a train in a coal mine.

It carries miners to the coal-face
where they work.

This can be a journey of several miles.

Other trains that take people to work

Because they can travel by train,
many people live far from their work.

In the mornings and evenings
the trains are packed.

During the rest of the day,
the trains are often nearly empty.

Trains people work in

In mail trains, men sort letters
as the train goes along.
The men work during the night.

Controlling the trains

Inside a modern signal box,
men control the movement of trains.

Moving lights on a board
show where the trains are.

The end of the 'Age of Steam'

Few countries now use
steam locomotives.

Most locomotives today are driven
by diesel engines or electric motors.

They are cheaper to run
and need less looking after.

Long-distance trains usually have
a separate locomotive to pull them.

Some small, local trains
have a diesel engine under the car.

Meals on trains

Long-distance trains have dining cars.
Canada had the first in 1867.

Beds on trains

For long journeys at night,
some carriages have beds in them.

The carriages are called sleeping cars.

A powerful, new locomotive

This American locomotive
is driven by a gas-turbine.

It works best on a long run,
pulling a heavy freight train.

Gas-turbine locomotives
are also used
to pull high speed passenger trains.

A train running on one rail

This train has rubber wheels.
They run on a concrete rail.
It is called a 'monorail',
meaning 'one rail'.
On some monorails,
the cars hang below the rail.

A famous Japanese railway

The new Tokaido line, in Japan, is more than 400 miles long. This modern electric train travels at more than 100 miles an hour.

44

A new British train

The APT (Advanced Passenger Train)
is the newest British train.

It can be driven by gas-turbines
or electric motors.

It can reach a speed
of 150 miles an hour.

Other ways of travelling

Nowadays, people can travel
by road and air as well as by rail.
The new trains will be comfortable
and fast to attract more passengers.

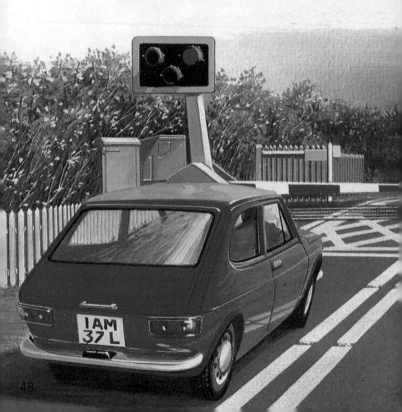

An early American wood-burning locomotive.

A steam locomotive of about 1875.

'Mallard'—
the world's fastest steam locomotive.

A diesel
locomotive.

An electric
locomotive.

The newest
British train.

The flanged rail of early railways

Early railways had this flange on the rail to keep the wheels on the track

The flanged wheels used on modern railways

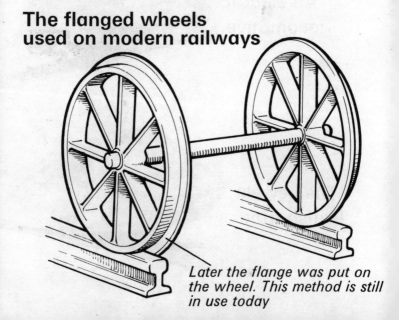

Later the flange was put on the wheel. This method is still in use today